A Boy's Will

FRED L. NEWHART JR. SCHOOL
25001 Oso Viejo
Mission Viejo, CA 92691

A Boy's Will

Erik Christian Haugaard

Illustrated by Troy Howell

Houghton Mifflin Company   Boston

Also by Erik Christian Haugaard

Hakon of Rogen's Saga
The Little Fishes
Orphans of the Wind
A Slave's Tale
A Messenger for Parliament
Cromwell's Boy
Chase Me, Catch Nobody!
Leif the Unlucky

Library of Congress Cataloging in Publication Data
Haugaard, Erik Christian.
A boy's will.

Summary: Patrick defies his unloving grandfather,
a smuggler of the Irish island of Valentia, by warning
John Paul Jones of the American fleet about an English ambush.
1. Jones, John Paul, 1747–1792–Juvenile fiction.
[1. Jones, John Paul, 1747–1792–Fiction]   I. Howell,
Troy, ill   II. Title.
PZ7.H286BO   1983   [Fic]   83-83
ISBN 0-395-33227-3

Printed in the United States of America

RNF ISBN 0-395-33227-3
PAP ISBN 0-395-54962-0

BP 10 9 8 7 6 5 4

A Boy's Will

The Boy

THE ISLAND OF VALENTIA, CALLED OILEAN DAIRBHRE by those who speak the Gaelic tongue, lies off the west coast of Ireland, in the County of Kerry. It makes a solid bulwark against the sea; and in its shelter, ships are protected from the might of the never-ending ocean that beats against its western shore. Once it had been a haven for those who sail the seas but seldom fly a flag.

By the year 1779 the pirates were gone, but smugglers still used this natural harbor. They sailed their small craft to France and brought back wine, spirits, and lace. Once or twice every summer, a brigantine would anchor up and stay for a week, showing the English colors to the seals, the dolphins, and the handful of people who lived there. With a few casks of brandy, the people of Valentia persuaded the English officers not to be too eager in carrying out their duties.

This time, however, the brigantine had not come alone, but was accompanied by four frigates.

Near the shore, a boy lay in the grass watching the small fleet. He saw the ship's boat pull away from the brigantine. An officer was being rowed ashore.

He will be coming to see my grandfather, Patrick thought angrily and stood up.

Patrick was a handsome boy, with long black hair that curled slightly and blue eyes. His eyes and hair were gifts from his mother. She had not managed to give him much else before she died. His father was dead, too; he had been lost at sea three years before, when the boy was only ten.

"Is your grandfather at home?" The English lieutenant's voice was harsh, a permanent trait from shouting commands.

"Aye, sir." Patrick knew the lieutenant well. He was the captain of the small brigantine, which was a very unimportant part of His Britannic Majesty, George the Third's fleet. "He has company," the boy said, grinning, for he thought the lieutenant had come to get some brandy from his grandfather, who was a smuggler.

"That suits me well enough." The lieutenant smiled. He had a liking for the boy because he had grown old in the service and never married; and now he knew that he would never have a child of his own. "What I have to say I would as soon all would hear."

Patrick pointed to the four frigates lying at anchor in the calm water. "Why are those big ships here?" he asked.

"The king has sent them to teach all rebels that

England still rules the seas around Ireland." The lieutenant ruffled the boy's hair; then he laughed. "Maybe they are here to teach your grandfather that he is not the king of Valentia."

"God's peace." The lieutenant's glance took in all six of the men who were seated around the peat fire.

"Would Your Honor care for something to take the chill off the evening?" Patrick's grandfather rose; his back was as straight as a young man's.

How small his eyes are. With that beak of a nose, he looks like a gull, Patrick thought; and his hand went to his face, as though he wanted to make sure of his own features.

"The commodore has sent me to inform you that no

ship is to sail from Valentia without his permission. To ensure that you should not misunderstand his order, he has asked me to tell you that there will be no warning shots. The first cannonball will go through the hull of your ships!"

"He must have fine gunners" – the boy's grandfather grinned – "to promise to sink us with the first shot."

The lieutenant's eyes were smarting from the smoke in the room. "As you know," he began, "the king is fighting a rebellion in his American colonies. We have reason to believe that one of these revolutionaries, a Scottish renegade named John Paul Jones, wanted for murder, has been given command of some ships supplied by His Majesty's enemy, France, with the purpose of harassing English shipping in these waters."

Even Patrick looked away from the lieutenant so that the officer could not guess from the expression on his face that they all had seen John Paul Jones. He had been more than once in Valentia.

The lieutenant coughed. "It is not that His Majesty doubts your loyalty, for some of you have kept your eyes open in foreign ports."

It is my grandfather who has played the spy, Patrick thought.

The lieutenant lifted his glass. "God save the king!"

Above the murmur of the other voices his grandfather's rose clearly, expressing that same wish.

The lieutenant's glass had contained some surprisingly good port wine, and he smiled good-naturedly as he left. Once outside, he paused. He was tempted to put his ear to the door and listen, but decided against it for fear of being observed.

A tall man with a patch over his right eye grumbled, "I would not like to see Master Jones caught."

"Then, Bill, you should get another patch to cover your good eye." The boy's grandfather chuckled at his own wit.

"Is his cause not ours?" the youngest man demanded angrily.

"Those Yankees are not fighting for the right to be smugglers! They want to govern themselves, my lads. And if they do, they'd hang people like us with as much pleasure as would the king. Besides, they are rebelling against tariffs – the very hand that feeds us! Every time the king puts a shilling on a keg of brandy, there's sixpence in it for us!" A murmur of approval greeted his grandfather's words.

Silently the boy stole from the cabin. It was late August. The setting sun had colored the clouds in the sky as pink as roses. The boy made his way to the eastern shore to see the English frigates once more, before nightfall. Their gunports were open. He counted the guns on the nearest vessel. Eighteen on the port side – thirty-six in all.

The ships had been anchored in lee of the land, so they could not be seen from the sea. On the approach to the anchorage was the small brigantine. She carried only sixteen guns. Her mast would be visible from afar. He understood it now. She was the bait!

Captain Jones would sight the brigantine; and when he sailed in to engage her, he would be met by four of the king's best-armed frigates. It was a cunningly laid trap. The boy always sided with the weak, and he wished passionately that somehow he could warn the rebel captain.

As he walked along the beach, Patrick thought of his mother. He could not even dimly remember her, yet no other person was so alive to him as she.

"She had never worn shoes until my son – the fool! – would marry her!" He had heard his grandfather shout this a hundred times, but the boy knew that in the old man's eyes his mother had committed an even worse crime than having been born so poor that she had

walked the earth barefoot. She had had her son baptized Patrick by one his grandfather called a "popish
vagabond."

For more than half a century the Roman Catholic
church had been all but forbidden in Ireland. Its priests
were hunted like foxes and had no more right to a
home there than the fox had to its den. Patrick did not
understand the differences between the king's church
and the pope's church, but he was made to suffer most
cruelly for them.

Many a beating had Patrick received from his grandfather, who thought that with a stick he could preach a
sermon on the boy's back to prove the worthlessness
of his mother. These forceful, painful attempts to
"whip the bad Catholic blood out of him" only made

the boy hate his grandfather and love that mother whom he had never known. Now, in some confused manner, John Paul Jones seemed to become his kin. "King George, is he not a tyrant like my grandfather?" the boy asked himself as he imagined the rebel captain on his ship, out on the sea.

As Patrick turned to cast one last glance at the frigates, he noticed a small boat near the shore. He knew it well, and that was why he had paid no attention to it before. It was the ship's boat for his grandfather's cutter, rigged with a lugsail. It was sixteen feet in length. Patrick had been out alone in it many a time.

"I could warn him," the boy whispered to himself.

From the pebbles at his feet, he chose the flattest stone. "If it skims six times, then I will sail out and warn him!"

He threw the little stone with all his might. Eight times it touched the calm water before it sank.

What Patrick's reasoning for setting out lacked in logic, his preparations made up for in good sense. As every seaman knows, in spite of being surrounded by an ocean of it, one should always have a good supply of water at hand. Behind a gorse bush, Patrick hid a jug of fresh water. Next he thought of provisions, since he might be at sea for several days. He would have to wait for his grandfather's guests to leave and for the old man himself to go to sleep.

It was midnight before Patrick and his grandfather were alone in the cottage.

"Paddy, my boy," the old man began good-humoredly, "though you are only half an Englishman, I believe that it is not all bogwater that runs in your veins. Here . . ." He poured a tumbler of brandy for the boy. "Let us drink to His Majesty! To war! And to even higher tariffs! And may our enemies catch the plague!"

The brandy burned Patrick's throat and made his eyes water; but he drank it all while his grandfather, who was watching him narrowly, laughed.

"Lend me your shoulder . . . Methinks the floor is moving like the deck of a ship in a gale." The old man leaned heavily on the boy as they walked the few steps to the other room. He had no sooner collapsed on the bed than he began to snore loudly.

Patrick covered him with a blanket. He had done this many times when the old smuggler had drunk too deeply of his own wares. Now the thought came to him that this might be the last time, and he stood gazing at his grandfather.

He was lying on his back, his head protruding from
the pillow like some ancient heathen image. His skin
had been polished by wind and weather till it resembled
wood more than living flesh. The boy raised his hand:
a gesture halfway between a wave and a salute.

His grandfather's larder supplied him with almost
a whole leg of roasted mutton, half a side of bacon,
a sack of potatoes, and a loaf of bread. These he packed
into a sailbag and stowed on top of them an iron pot
and his grandfather's tinderbox. Then he climbed the
ladder to the attic. For once, the trap door did not
squeak. There in a chest packed with his mother's
belongings was her cloak. It smelled musty, but it was
heavy and closely woven. It would keep him warm,
for even in summer it is cold at night on the sea. Now
he deemed himself ready and slung the bag over his
shoulder.

As he closed the door of the house, he realized for the first time that if he were successful in his quest, he would never be able to enter it again. He fondled the latch. This was, after all, his home. Then with a sigh he turned and started toward the shore, where the little boat was waiting for him.

The Island

PATRICK MADE A STRANGE FIGURE, WALKING DOWN to the beach with the big sailbag over one shoulder and his mother's black cloak over the other. When he put his burdens down, he looked out toward His Majesty's frigates, four large vessels etched like silhouettes against the clear night air. Only one small cloud was drifting toward the moon. The breeze was slight and from the northeast, which was fair for him.

The little boat was kept on a running mooring; a stake had been driven into the ground above the beach. Patrick loosened the rope and pulled on it. The boat obeyed and silently glided toward shore. When its keel touched the stony beach, the boy rolled up his trousers and carried his provisions on board. Then he shoved the boat out as far as he could without untying the painter, with which it was attached to the mooring.

The cloud was nearing the moon. Once more the boy glanced at the frigates. He knew that the watch on board had been given orders to keep a sharp eye out to make sure none of the smugglers slipped away; but he hoped that they would not notice a boat as small as his.

The cloud was now very near the moon. Patrick undid the bits of rope that were fastened around the sail. As the moon disappeared behind the cloud, he grabbed the halyard and pulled up the sail. The spar and canvas were very heavy, and he had to use all his strength. At last, he untied the painter and cast off.

The wind was light, but the tide was with him. In the sound between Valentia and the mainland, the current is swift, especially at the narrowest point. At any moment he expected to hear a sailor on one of the men-of-war sing out that he had been discovered.

The moon broke free from the cloud before he reached the headland; and pointless as it was, he ducked and made himself as small as possible. Here there were rocks and he had to steer farther out into the sound. The strong tide caught him and the boat moved swiftly.

Finally, when the frigates disappeared from his sight, he felt the coldness of the night, and, leaving the helm for a moment, he wrapped himself in his mother's cloak. The wind came from behind. As he let out the sail a little, he smiled; he would be past Port Magee and out in the open sea before sunrise.

There was but a glimmer of light from the east when the boy's boat glided past the village named after the famous smuggler Magee. As the little boat cleared the tip of the island and the land to port disappeared, Patrick saw an ocean that lay smooth as a lake.

The sun was rising and the mountains of Kerry glowed. The boy set a course for Skelling Michael, that island rock that rises seven hundred feet out of a sea so deep that there is no anchorage near its shore. Long ago there had been a monastery here. And it is said that the great Norse king, Olaf Trygveson, had been made a Christian and baptized in this desolate place.

Patrick had been on the island only once, for it is dangerous to sail close to it except in fair weather. But as he scanned the empty horizon, hoping to see the American rebel ships, it occurred to him to land there,

because from the summit of the island he would be able to spy any approaching ship long before it could be seen by the watch of the English men-of-war at Valentia.

The wind freshened, and he sailed through a flock of puffins. Although it was August, a few of them still had brightly colored beaks. The little birds did not fly away. They seemed not to be frightened at all, and waited to dive until the bow of the boat was only a few feet away from them.

As he neared Skelling Michael, the breeze weakened, and finally his sail hung slack. The boat no longer obeyed the helm. Even when the great ocean appears still, there is movement within it. Like the breast of a great giant sleeping, it heaves. The sail swung from one side of the boat to the other, flapping noisily.

Patrick lowered it, and taking the jug of water, the bread, and the leg of mutton with him into the stern, he settled himself and began to eat.

The heat of the sun that was now high in the sky made him sleepy. He dozed. In his dream, his grandfather appeared. The old man was running after him, pursuing him across a wide, sandy beach. The boy felt as if he were running for his life. Faster and faster his feet fled over the sand, yet the old smuggler was gaining on him. He could hear him breathing right behind him; but at the very moment that his grandfather's clawlike hand was about to grasp his shoulder, he woke up. The dream was over and he could see the clear blue sky through his half-opened eyes, yet he still could hear the breathing of his pursuer!

For a moment he lay motionless, then slowly he turned his head. There, near the stern of the boat, not more than a few feet away, was a porpoise. The little whale was enjoying the warm sun. The strange rumbling sound came when it expelled the air from its lungs. Patrick jumped to his feet, rocking the boat; and the porpoise dived out of sight.

Skelling Michael towered ahead of him: the pointed top of a great mountain whose base is lost in the depths of the sea.

The oars were heavy, meant for a man not a boy, but now Patrick was eager to land and he started to row.

It took him almost an hour to reach that cut in the rock called Blind Man's Cove. This was the place the monks had used when bringing supplies to their monastery. It faces east and thus is sheltered from the west wind. Still, it is a poor landing, because if there

is a swell running, the waves will hammer a boat against the rocks.

That day the waters were like glass, and Patrick's gaze could follow the bending rays of the sun as they penetrated the depths. Painter in hand, he jumped ashore and fastened the rope around a rock; then he pulled on it, to make sure it would hold. Now it was high tide, and he gave his boat a little push to find out whether he had given it rope enough for the falling tide. The little vessel floated halfway across the tiny cove toward the cliff face. He decided it would be safe enough and started along the path to the summit.

Hundreds of years ago, the monks had cut steps into the rock. Wind and rain had worn them; one had to climb with care or else one might fall. Patrick was as agile and sure-footed as a little goat, yet as he mounted the rude stairs, he kept his glance at his feet. He had promised himself that if he did not look up until he reached the top, he would see the ships of John Paul Jones.

But even from the high perch of the monastery sight, the sea was empty. He turned and looked back toward Valentia and the mainland. The coastline of the island was lost in a haze. Nearby was the little Skelling. It has almost the same contours as Skelling Michael but is only half the size.

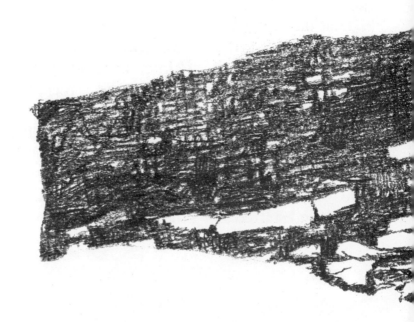

To the south, he could see Bull Rock; and to the north, he could make out the Blasket Islands floating like blue shadows on the ocean. The air was magically

still; the voice of the sea was mute; and only the cries of the gulls could be heard. He had been told by the old woman who had cared for him when he was small that it was here, on this very spot, that St. Patrick had fought the last battle against the evil and venomous serpents that long ago had infested Ireland. With the aid of St. Michael he had cast them into the sea; and therefore the Great Skelling was the most holy place to which an Irishman could make a pilgrimage.

Patrick explored the ruins of the buildings abandoned by the monks centuries before. On the wall of what he thought must have been a church was a rude cross. Patrick sank to his knees in front of it and prayed.

"Lord protect me!" he repeated over and over again. But as he knelt on the stone floor, it was not God but his grandfather who appeared before him. When the boy closed his eyes, he saw the old man's countenance; it was hard and condemning.

A breeze sprang up; it was from land. Patrick was enough of a seaman to know that it was but an evening breeze, which would die as soon as the sun set. For the last time he looked out over the endless sea. There were no ships in sight.

Before he slowly descended the steps, he gathered straw on the tiny plateau, which was the only place on the island where anything but sea pinks grew. It was well dried, for it had not rained for almost a week. At Blind Man's Cove he found, in the crevices between the rocks, branches and splinters of wood that the waves had deposited there. On a flat stone, he built

a little fire. As he handled his grandfather's tinderbox, he thought how angry the old man would be when he discovered that it was gone.

Patrick boiled potatoes and chunks of bacon. When he had finished eating, he tried to keep the fire going, but soon his little pile of wood was gone; only the embers were left. He warmed his hands over them; then he pulled his little boat alongside the rocks and climbed on board. Wrapping himself in his mother's cloak, he lay down on the floorboards to sleep.

The boy looked up at the stars. They were to him the most beautiful sight of all. He believed that his mother was among them. He picked out the star that he thought shone the brightest, then mumbled, "I am here, Mother. I am here." Just at that moment a shooting star fell, and Patrick smiled. His mother had heard him.

When he woke in the morning, he knew immediately that there had been a change in the weather. The boat was rocking gently, and tiny waves were lapping at the rocks. The sun was well above the horizon. Like a dog he shook himself, and leaning over the gunwale of the boat, he washed his face. He combed his hair with his hands, and his morning toilet was finished.

Munching a piece of bread, he climbed once more toward the summit of the island. This time he told himself that he would not see the rebel ships; and when he reached the point where he could look westward, he hardly dared lift his head.

There they were! Five of them, with all canvas spread, bearing down upon Valentia!

The Race

THE HULLS OF THE FIVE SHIPS WERE JUST VISIBLE ABOVE THE horizon. Three of them were frigates, but the other two were smaller than the brigantine that the English were using as bait. The squadron was larger than the boy had expected.

"They would give the English a fair fight," he whispered to himself, "but only if they were warned, so they could sail into Valentia with decks cleared and gunports open!"

Patrick waited only a moment to make certain of the American rebel ships' course, then he ran down to the cove.

The sail flapped lazily as he hoisted it. He was in lee of the island, and the wind was from the southwest, so he would have to row; but a hundred yards from the island, the wind caught him and he pulled in his oars.

It was a perfect breeze, and his boat heeled over as it cut through the little waves. He was sailing close to the wind, steering west; thus he hoped to cut the course of John Paul Jones's squadron.

Skelling Michael was well astern when the boy by chance glanced toward Valentia. A cutter had just passed the headland and was standing out to sea. He knew the ship well. Had he not sailed on her to Brittany? It was his grandfather's boat!

He should have known that the English commodore's spy would easily gain permission to leave Valentia. At first Patrick felt only fear, as though his grandfather had already caught him and he were waiting for the beating that he knew must follow. But then, as he hauled the sail tighter and steered even closer to the wind, he felt a strange joy. Oh, it was fitting enough, he thought to himself, that he and the old smuggler should race.

His grandfather's boat, the *Bonny Anne*, was a fifty-ton cutter. She was a fast ship, as many a revenue boat, through the years, had learned; but as she was several miles to the north, the direction of the wind would not allow her to keep the same course as Patrick. She would have to turn a few times before she could catch up with him.

As he drew near, Patrick realized that two of the rebel frigates were smaller than the ones anchored at Valentia; only the largest of the ships John Paul Jones commanded might carry as many guns as His Majesty's men-of-war. And the smaller boats were merely a cutter and a corvette. Neither had more than ten gunports.

Close-hauled, her sails drawn as tight as possible, the *Bonny Anne* was sweeping down toward him. Still, she would cross his course half a mile astern, and by that time he would be very near the American ships.

Patrick's little boat shot through the sea and left a wake of foam behind it. The breeze was freshening. If any more wind came, he would not be able to hold his course. There would be no time to reef; he would have to let out the sail and spill the wind.

The waves were growing in strength and size, even though there was not yet enough wind to raise much of a sea. As its bow cleaved the waves, spray flew in over Patrick's boat. Often when he had sailed in the

Bonny Anne, he had lain on the deck near the bowsprit, laughing as the spray washed his face; but now he was worried. If he shipped too much water, all would be lost. His grandfather would be able to pick him up like an apple that had fallen from a tree. He could now see the figures of the men on board the rebel ships. Were they watching him? Would they notice if he signaled to them?

The *Bonny Anne* had turned and was now forging ahead on the same course as himself. She had all sails set: flying jib, jib, staysail, mainsail, and topsail. The breeze, which was just right for her, was beginning to be too much for Patrick's small craft. She was about half a mile behind him and gaining fast.

The boy looked back. There, standing in the bow and shaking his fist, was his grandfather. But now Patrick did not give a thought to the beating that fist promised – though he knew it would come if

he were overtaken, as surely as night follows day. He was pitting his will against his grandfather's; and he believed that if he did not win this race, nothing would matter anymore.

After his father's death, Patrick had been brought to his grandfather's house. Had the old man shown him some kindness, he would readily have won his heart, for in truth, the boy admired the old smuggler. Had he at least let his daughter-in-law rest peacefully in her grave, he might not now be in a furious race with her son. But he had cursed Patrick's mother, blaming her for every misfortune, even the failings of her husband. It was as if he were jealous of that poor dead girl and wanted his grandson to choose between them. Well, the boy had chosen, and now the old man was shaking his fist in rage and swearing that he would kill him.

The squadron was drawing close, but so was the *Bonny Anne*. Patrick was steering toward the largest of the ships, for surely that must be the flagship of Captain Jones. One of the smaller frigates was nearer, but he thought he might pass astern of her.

A wave a little larger than the others sent bucketfuls of water into his boat.

As he expected, he passed aft of the small frigate. At the taffrail many men were standing and watching. Frantically, Patrick waved to them; they waved back, amused at the race between the small boat and the cutter.

Now the largest of the rebel ships was slightly to

port, and the *Bonny Anne* was less than a hundred yards behind him. The boy clenched the tiller so hard that his knuckles showed white. He would sail in front of the ship if he could, then go about, hoping to make the sailors understand that they must throw him a line.

Only when it was too late did he realize that he would not pass the bow of the ship but collide with her!

Quickly he glanced back; the *Bonny Anne* was falling off and would sail astern of the larger vessel.

Several of the sailors on the great frigate were waving their arms wildly and shouting to Patrick to go about.

The boy pulled the sheet even tighter in a last desperate effort to make his boat sail even closer to the wind and pass in front of the man-of-war, but it was in vain. The bow of Captain Jones's flagship crushed the gunwale and two of the planks of his little boat, and immediately it was swamped. Had it turned over, Patrick would have drowned, but the water-filled wreck glided alongside the hull of the ship.

A sailor with more sense than his comrades threw a line to the boy, and Patrick grabbed it. One minute he was in his boat and the next he was being dragged through the whirling sea by the speeding ship. As his head emerged from the water, he managed to get the end of the rope between his legs. For one terrible moment, when he was being pulled up, he thought he would have to let go because of the pain when the knuckles of his hands scraped against the planks of the hull.

Patrick was hauled over the railing and the sailors flocked around him. "What kind of fish have we caught?" one of them asked.

When he had breath enough, the boy said slowly, "I must speak to Captain Jones."

"A talking fish!" the man shouted, and all the sailors laughed.

"Make way," a voice commanded; and instantly everyone obeyed.

"It is Commodore Jones," the sailor who had thrown Patrick the line now whispered to him.

Unsteadily the boy started to get up; his hands were bleeding.

"What tomfoolery is this?" John Paul Jones said sternly. "It is but luck that you were not drowned."

"I have come, sir, to warn you . . . But my grandfather would not have it."

The boy's mention of his grandfather made Commodore Jones smile; he, too, had been watching the race between the cutter and the small boat. "Warn me of what?" he asked kindly.

"There is an English squadron hidden behind Valentia Island," he explained, pointing toward the bow of the ship and the coast beyond it.

"How many ships are there?" The man wrinkled his brow as if he were contemplating whether or not the boy spoke the truth.

"Four frigates and a brigantine. She is anchored in the offing for you to see, sir."

"We have observed the brigantine and wondered what she was doing seeking such a poor anchorage." The commodore smiled. "How many guns do the frigates carry?"

"Thirty-six, sir. They are fine ships."

John Paul Jones was staring intently toward the island. Should he keep his course and engage the English? With a sigh, he dismissed the idea; it would be foolhardy, not courageous. If I had but one frigate more and could depend on the commander of the *Alliance*, he thought as he looked to starboard at that ship, a few cables' lengths ahead of him; then he shook his head. "Change course due north and order the others to follow us," he ordered. An officer who was standing nearby saluted and walked away.

The boy sniffled; he was drenched and cold.

"What is your name?" the commodore asked.

"Patrick, sir."

"Patrick, I thank you!" John Paul Jones made a little bow. "It is a good name. We shall brag that we were saved by a saint. Will you sail with us? This"—his hand swept out over the sea—"is the Continental Navy."

The boy bowed. He did not know what "continental" meant, but he answered loud and clear, "I will."

Commodore Jones smiled and examined the boy's face as if he wanted to remember every one of his features. "Take him below to my cabin and find him some dry clothes," he said before he walked forward.

"Come with me." The sailor who had already befriended Patrick took his hand, as if he were afraid that he might fall; but the boy walked to the railing. His grandfather's cutter was far away, sailing toward Valentia. At that moment, he felt certain that he would never see the island again.

"It is a great thing that you did." The sailor was smiling as he gently put his arm around the boy's shoulder to guide him below.

"A great thing." Patrick repeated the words. Why had he done it? Now his mother would be alone in the graveyard, back there on that storm-torn coast; and suddenly he remembered that he had lost her cloak.

"You are a hero," the sailor said as he helped the boy down the ladderlike stairs.

When they reached the great cabin of the *Bonhomme Richard*, Patrick felt so weak that he nearly fell. He let the sailor undress him as if he were a little child; and though he said to himself several times, "I won the race," he could not keep the tears from running down his face.